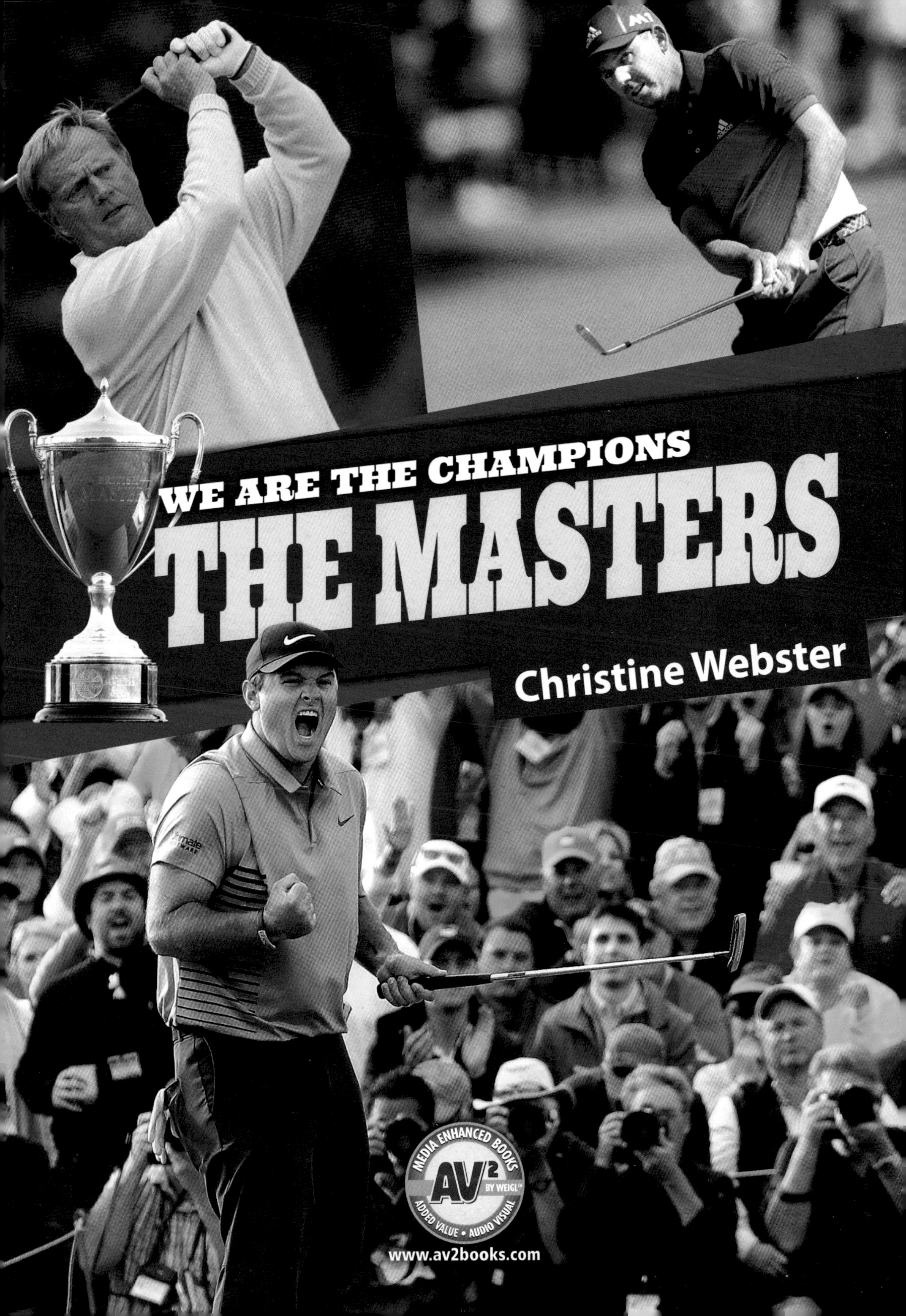

WE ARE THE CHAMPIONS

THE MASTERS

Christine Webster

AV² provides enriched content that supplements and complements this book. Weigl's AV² books strive to create inspired learning and engage young minds in a total learning experience.

Your AV² Media Enhanced books come alive with...

Audio
Listen to sections of the book read aloud.

Key Words
Study vocabulary, and complete a matching word activity.

Video
Watch informative video clips.

Quizzes
Test your knowledge.

Embedded Weblinks
Gain additional information for research.

Slide Show
View images and captions, and prepare a presentation.

Try This!
Complete activities and hands-on experiments.

... and much, much more!

Go to **www.av2books.com**, and enter this book's unique code.

BOOK CODE

A V E 8 8 6 5 5

AV² by Weigl brings you media enhanced books that support active learning.

Published by AV² by Weigl
350 5th Avenue, 59th Floor
New York, NY 10118
Website: www.av2books.com

Library of Congress Control Number: 2018965260

ISBN 978-1-7911-0056-8 (hardcover)
ISBN 978-1-7911-0582-2 (softcover)
ISBN 978-1-7911-0058-2 (single-user eBook)
ISBN 978-1-7911-0057-5 (multi-user eBook)

Printed in Brainerd, Minnesota, United States
1 2 3 4 5 6 7 8 9 0 22 21 20 19 18

122018
102318

Project Coordinator: Jared Siemens
Art Director: Terry Paulhus

Every reasonable effort has been made to trace ownership and to obtain permission to reprint copyright material. The publishers would be pleased to have any errors or omissions brought to their attention so that they may be corrected in subsequent printings. Weigl acknowledges Getty Images and Alamy as its primary image suppliers for this title.

WE ARE THE CHAMPIONS

THE MASTERS

HOLE	1	2	3	4	5	6	7	8	9	10	11	12	13	14	15	16	17	18
PAR	4	5	4	3	4	3	4	5	4	4	4	3	5	4	5	3	4	4
		8	9	9	9	10	10	10										
SPIETH																		
ROSE		5	6	6														
HOFFMAN		4	6	6	6													
DAY		5	6	6	6	5	5	4	5	5	5	4	3	3				
ELS		4	5	4	4													
GARCIA																		
OOSTHU																		

CONTENTS

3

What Is the Masters Golf Tournament?

The Masters is a 72-hole golf tournament that takes place over four days in April each year. It is held at the Augusta National Golf Club in Georgia. Since 1940, the Masters has been the first major golf championship of the year. It is one of the four most important golf tournaments in the world.

Changes through the Years

After a very successful golf career, champion golfer Bobby Jones decided to retire from playing the sport professionally in 1930. Jones and his business partner, Clifford Roberts, wanted to establish a new golf course with a national membership. The men paid $70,000 for a 365-acre (142-hectare) property in Augusta, Georgia. They hired a Scottish architect, Alister Mackenzie, to design the course. Construction began on the site in 1931, and the following year it opened with a limited amount of playing area. The completed course officially opened in 1933. Today, Augusta National Golf Club is one of the best-known golf courses in the world, known for its beauty and challenging play.

There are more than **15,000 golf courses** in the United States.

The prize at the **first** Masters, held in 1934 in Augusta, was **$1,500**, which is worth about **$28,000** today.

The game of golf originated in **Scotland** in the mid-1400s.

When construction was complete, Jones invited a select group of his friends to play on the new course. He challenged them to a friendly tournament, beginning the tradition that led to the Masters Golf Tournament. Thousands flock to Augusta to watch the tournament in person. Millions of other people watch the event on television.

PAST

The first golf balls were made from three pieces of leather that were covered in feathers.

Golf consisted of 13 rules.

Club shafts were made out of wood.

Irons, or clubs used for medium-distance shots, had smooth faces.

PRESENT

Golf balls are made of **synthetic** materials and are dimpled to help them travel farther.

There are 34 rules.

Shafts are made from a special type of steel or **graphite**.

Irons have grooved faces.

The History

Jones challenged his friends to a tournament at the new course. The tournament was so much fun that Jones and Roberts decided to make it an annual event. The first official event took place in March, 1934, and was called the Augusta National Invitation Tournament. Horton Smith won the event. Five years later, the name was officially changed to the Masters Golf Tournament.

For three years during World War II (1939–1945), the Masters Tournament was not played. Instead, cattle and turkeys were raised on the grounds. After World War II, the Masters Golf Tournament gained popularity with the help of television coverage. People also enjoyed watching a rising star, Arnold Palmer, play the game. Palmer won the tournament four times between 1958 and 1964. The growing popularity of the Masters Tournament gave it a place as one of the four major professional golfing events.

During the 1980s, people from countries other than the United States began winning the tournament, including Seve Ballesteros of Spain, who claimed the title twice. However, American golf legend Jack Nicklaus won the tournament six times from 1963 to 1986. He remains the golfer with the most Masters championships.

Arnold Palmer won seven major golf championships. He was inducted into the World Golf Hall of Fame in 1974.

Bob Goalby competed in the Masters 27 years in a row from 1960 to 1986. He won the tournament in 1968.

Though more than 70 years have passed since Jones held the first tournament at Augusta National Golf Club, many of its original traditions have remained in place. For example, only men can play in the event, and the only way for players to take part is to be invited. In most cases, the world's top amateur and professional male golfers are invited to play each year. In 2002, the National Council of Women's Organizations challenged the Augusta National Club to accept female members. The club refused to change its policy. It decided to remain a male-only club.

AUGUSTA'S FEATURES

The Augusta National Golf Club is considered one of the most beautiful golf courses in the world. It has many notable natural features. For example, President Eisenhower hit his ball into the pine tree at the 17th hole so many times that he asked for the tree to be cut down. Today, it is known as the Eisenhower Tree. Another example is Rae's Creek. The lowest point on the course, the creek was named after the land's former owner, John Rae. It flows along several holes and has bridges crossing it in two places. Augusta National Golf Club is also known for being very neat and tidy. In fact, the green color of napkins handed out with refreshments matches the grass perfectly. This is so that if one of the napkins falls to the ground, it will blend in with the grass.

The Rules

Like any sport, golf has rules of the game. There are two main points to know before beginning a game of golf. First, the course must be played as it is when a player arrives. If there has been a hard rain, the ground will be mushy. On a hot summer day, the ground may be hard and dry. Second, the ball must be played from the place where it lands. It cannot be moved to another location. There are special clubs to hit a ball out of a sandy or rough area. If the ball lands in the water, a new ball can be used, but the player will lose a stroke.

1
The Long Game

Players start a round of golf in the tee box, a long way from the small hole they are shooting for. Players use clubs called drivers to try to hit the ball as close to the hole as possible. The score is determined by the number of shots a golfer takes before the ball lands in the hole.

2
Fairways

Once the ball is hit off the tee, it travels along the fairway. The grass is closely cropped along this area that runs between the tee and the green of a golf hole. Players use clubs called irons on the fairway. Irons do not hit the ball as far as drivers, but they offer more accurate aim.

3

Putting Green

Putting is the act of hitting the ball into the hole. To putt, the golfer gently strikes the ball with a club called a putter. Players putt the ball on the putting green. This is a well-groomed grassy area surrounding the hole. The grass here is mowed shorter than any other part of the course.

4

Scoring

In a golf game, the person with the lowest score is the winner. Each time a golfer hits the ball, it counts as one stroke. At the end of each hole, the number of strokes the golfer used to sink the ball are recorded. At the end of the game, the total is tallied. This is the golfer's score. Par refers to the number of strokes it should take a golfer to complete the hole. If a hole is par four, it should take four strokes to sink the ball.

		HOLE	1	2	3	4	5	6	7	8	9	10	11	12	13	14	15
		PAR	4	5	4	3	4	3	4	5	4	4	4	3	5	4	5
8	SPIETH		8	9	9	9	10	10	10								
5	ROSE																
5	HOFFMAN		5	6	6												
5	DAY		4	6	6	6											
5	ELS		5	6	6	6	5	5	4	5	5	4	3	3			
4	GARCIA		4	5	4	4											
0	OOSTHUIZEN		1	2	2	2	3	3	3	4	4	4	3				

LEADERS

5

Etiquette

Etiquette is one of the most important parts of the game of golf. Players are expected to behave in a certain way during a game. For example, if a golfer makes a hole, or divot, in the ground when hitting the ball, that person should repair the grass for the next player. Noise should be kept to a minimum on the course. Golf requires concentration, and loud sounds, talking, and sudden movements can distract players. Golf carts should be driven along paths so as not to damage the course. The player with the best score from the previous hole gets to tee off first at the next hole.

MAKING THE CALL

Unlike most sports, golf does not require an official to make calls throughout the game. However, during a golf tournament, a referee usually determines if the rules of the game are being followed during a tournament. The referee decides if any rules have been broken, and if so, what sort of action to take. An observer is a person who has been appointed to assist a referee.

The Golf Course

Golf courses usually are found on a large piece of land that is about 6,000 to 7,000 yards (5,500 to 6,400 meters) long from the first tee to the last hole. The land is divided into 18 sections, also called holes, that vary from about 100 to 600 yards (90 to 550 m) in length. Each hole has a starting point, called a tee. The land around the tee is level and higher than the rest of the land in the area.

The fairway is a long stretch of land, about 30 to 100 yards (27 to 90 m) wide. Here, the grass is cut very short to give a good playing surface. On each side of the fairway is an area called the rough. The rough is not well kept, and there are natural obstacles, such as tall grass, bushes, trees, sand, or marsh, to challenge the golfer. Sometimes, man-made obstacles are placed on the course. These are called bunkers or traps. They can be hollows in the ground filled with sand or similar material, or they can be mounds, ditches, or ponds.

At the farthest end of the fairway is the putting green. It has closely cropped grass surrounding a hole in the ground. A plastic or metal cup is placed inside the hole, which is about 4.25 inches (10.8 centimeters) in diameter and about 4 inches (10 cm) deep. A flag marks the location of the hole so that golfers know where to aim when they hit the ball off the tee. Each hole is given a number from 1 to 18. A full-sized golf course has 18 holes, though smaller ones may only have nine.

PLAYING THE GAME

There are two basic kinds of golf games. They are called match play and stroke play. In match play, the winner is the person who scores the lowest on the most holes. Overall, this person's score may be higher than another player's. In stroke play, the winner is the player who uses the least number of strokes in the entire game. The Master Tournament uses stroke play rules.

AUGUSTA NATIONAL
GOLF CLUB COURSE MAP

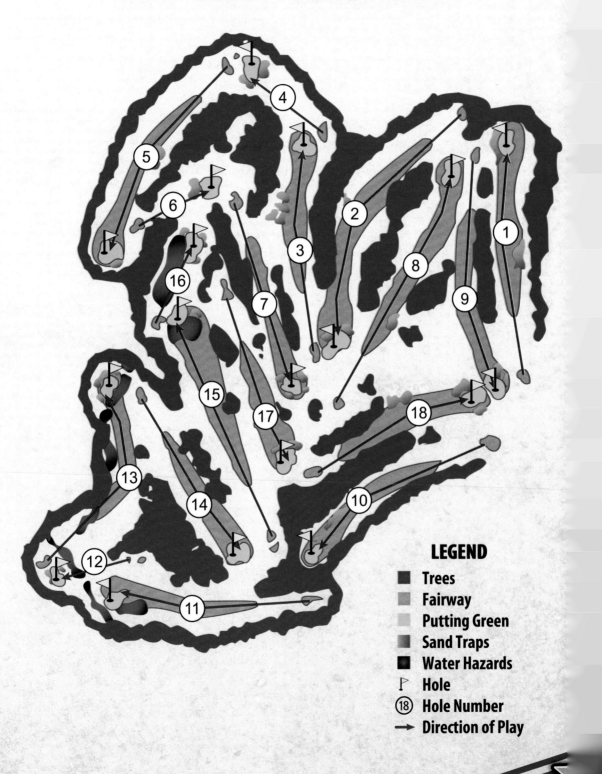

LEGEND

- Trees
- Fairway
- Putting Green
- Sand Traps
- Water Hazards
- ⚑ Hole
- ⑱ Hole Number
- → Direction of Play

Golf Equipment

The main pieces of equipment for a golfer are clubs and a ball. There are three main types of clubs—woods, irons, and putters. Woods and irons come in many shapes and sizes that are used in different situations. Most players carry their clubs and other gear in a golf bag. Professional golfers are allowed to carry up to 14 clubs during a game.

Woods are used when a player needs to shoot the ball a long distance. Most often, these shots are taken from the tee or a part of the fairway that is a long distance from the putting green.

Irons are used to make precise shots from the fairway. Players use irons called wedges to hit their ball out of traps or the rough when they are near the green. Putters are used when the ball has a short distance to travel to reach the hole.

Golf tees are another important piece of golf equipment. The golf ball is balanced on a tee before players take their first shot on any hole. Usually, tees are made from wood or plastic. They look similar to a nail, with a cup-shaped head for the ball to rest on.

Wood

Iron

Putter

Golf Bag

Clothing is important in a golf game. Most courses require golfers to dress according to a dress code. Often, players are not allowed to wear jeans, T-shirts, or shorts. Most golfers wear a collared shirt and dress pants.

Special shoes with spikes on the soles are worn to give the golfer a good grip on the grass. Many golfers also wear a glove on one hand to help them grip the club and prevent **blistering**.

Hat

Club

Glove

Shoes

GOLF BALLS

Golf balls come in many colors, sizes, and weights. For official play, a ball cannot measure less than 1.68 inches (42.67 millimeters) in diameter or weigh more than 1.62 ounces (45.93 grams). About 100 years ago, it became known that scratched balls traveled farther than smooth balls. This is where the idea came from to put dents, or dimples, on the surface of golf balls. Golf balls today have 330 to 500 dimples. They help the ball move more easily through the air. During a game, players may request a ball with a different number of dimples. The best golf balls have between 380 to 432 dimples.

Qualifying to Play

It can take years for a player to qualify to receive an invitation to the Masters. After playing as amateur golfers in various championships, the best players go on to play the sport professionally. Once they have played in and won major tournaments, such as the British Open, the PGA Championship, the U.S. Open, The Players Championship, or the U.S. Amateur Championship, they gain recognition as serious competitors. The Masters Committee reviews the winners of these events to determine who should be invited to play at the Augusta course in April.

There are many factors involved in being able to play in the Masters Golf Tournament. Each year, players who meet certain criteria receive an automatic invitation. In some cases, the Masters Committee will invite other players that do not qualify officially. Typically, this is done for international players.

Rickie Fowler competed in the Masters every year between 2011 and 2017. A PGA Deutsche Bank Championship win helped get him there in 2015.

MASTERS
TUESDAY
April 3, 2018

Tickets for the Masters are sold by application only. Applicants who receive tickets are selected randomly.

The Masters has the smallest group of players out of all the major golf championships. Only about 90 players are invited to compete in this tournament. In most tournaments, golfers play in groups of four. However, during the Masters, golfers play in groups of three for the first 36 holes, or the first two days of the tournament. After this, some players are cut from the competition. Players that are not within 44 places of the lead or are more than 10 strokes behind the 36-hole score set by the leader are eliminated from the rest of the tournament.

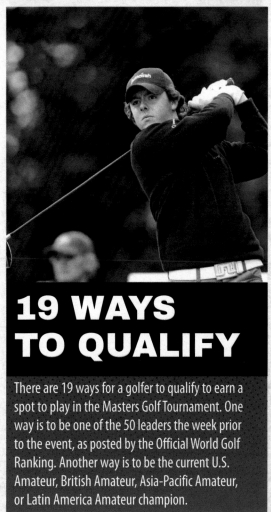

19 WAYS TO QUALIFY

There are 19 ways for a golfer to qualify to earn a spot to play in the Masters Golf Tournament. One way is to be one of the 50 leaders the week prior to the event, as posted by the Official World Golf Ranking. Another way is to be the current U.S. Amateur, British Amateur, Asia-Pacific Amateur, or Latin America Amateur champion.

The Main Event

Unlike other major golf championships, the Masters is held in the same location each year. The Augusta National Golf Club is one of the most **exclusive** golf clubs in the world. Bobby Jones, Clifford Roberts, and Alister MacKenzie worked on the course with Scotland as their inspiration.

The Augusta National Golf Club is known for its beautiful landscaping. Natural flowers, trees, and shrubs are found all over the course. To showcase this feature, in 1940, the date for the tournament was changed from March to the first full week in April. By this time each year, the flowers and shrubs at the course are in full bloom. Each hole on the course is named after a tree or shrub found nearby.

The greens at the Augusta National Golf Club were originally made from **Bermuda grass**. They were reconstructed in 1981, and **bent grass** replaced the Bermuda grass. Deep green in color, bent grass is thick and low-growing, with a smooth surface.

The Augusta National Golf Club is an exclusive club. It has only about 300 members. Like the tournament, the only way to become a member is by invitation. Women have been able to join only since 2012.

For members who want to stay on site, the Crow's Nest is a living space for up to five people. It is one room with partitions to divide it into three spaces, each with a bed. A full bathroom, sitting area, television, and telephone are also found here.

Augusta National Golf Club **fees** range from **$25,000 to $50,000** per year.

A Masters winner only receives **one jacket**, even if they win the championship multiple times.

At least **five** different types of **pine trees** grow around the Augusta golf course.

MASTERS GOLF TOURNAMENT WINNERS
2010–2018

YEAR	PLAYER	FINAL	ROUND 1	ROUND 2	ROUND 3	ROUND 4	STROKES	EARNINGS
2018	Patrick Reed	-15	69	66	67	71	273	$1,980,000
2017	Sergio Garcia	-9	71	69	70	69	279	$1,980,000
2016	Danny Willett	-5	70	74	72	67	283	$1,800,000
2015	Jordan Spieth	-18	64	66	70	70	270	$1,800,000
2014	Bubba Watson	-8	69	68	74	69	280	$1,620,000
2013	Adam Scott	-9	69	72	69	69	279	$1,440,000
2012	Bubba Watson	-10	69	71	70	68	278	$1,440,000
2011	Charl Schwartzel	-14	69	71	68	66	274	$1,440,000
2010	Phil Mickelson	-16	67	71	67	67	272	$1,350,000

THE GREEN JACKET

In 1937, the Augusta National Golf Club designed a members-only coat. The jackets were bought from the Brooks Uniform Company in New York. Members were told to wear the jackets during the Masters Golf Tournament. This was so that other people would be able to easily identify them. At first, the members did not like the idea of wearing the heavy, green coat. A new design, years later, made it more comfortable to wear in the Georgia heat.

The jacket was given to the winner of the Masters Golf Tournament for the first time in 1949. The green jacket had an Augusta National Golf Club logo on the left chest pocket and on each brass button. It is tradition for the previous winner to help the new winner put on the jacket for the first time. The winner keeps the jacket for one year before returning the jacket to the club. Whenever the returning champion visits, the jacket is there for him to wear.

Since 1961, the Masters Trophy is also awarded to the champion. It has a model of the Augusta clubhouse mounted on a pedestal. The main trophy remains at the club, but since 1993, a sterling silver copy has been given to the champion, along with a gold medal.

The Masters Golf Tournament is one of four major golf tournaments worldwide. The three other tournaments are the U.S. Open, the British Open, and the PGA Championship. Golfers are only considered among golf's greatest players when they have won one of these major tournaments. When a player wins all four tournaments, they are said to have won the Grand Slam of golf. Only one player has ever won all four majors in the same year. This was done by Bobby Jones in 1930.

United Kingdom, British Open

1 2018—Carnoustie Golf Links, Carnoustie, Angus, Scotland

2 2017—Royal Birkdale Golf Club, Southport, Merseyside, England

3 2016—Royal Troon Golf Club, Troon, Ayrshire, Scotland

4 2015—The Old Course, St Andrews Links, Fife, Scotland

5 2014—Royal Liverpool Golf Club, Hoylake, Wirral, England

SCALE

0 miles   115 miles

0 km   186 km

CANADA

Maine
New Hampshire
Vermont
Massachusetts
Rhode Island
Connecticut

North Dakota
Minnesota
Wisconsin
South Dakota
Michigan
New York
Pennsylvania
New Jersey
Delaware
Maryland
District of Columbia
Iowa
Ohio
Nebraska
Indiana
Illinois
West Virginia
Virginia
Kansas
Missouri
Kentucky
North Carolina
Tennessee
Oklahoma
South Carolina
Arkansas
Georgia
Alabama
Florida
Texas
Louisiana

Atlantic Ocean

SCALE
0 miles   360 miles
0 kilometers   580 km

MAP LEGEND
- United States
- United Kingdom
- Other Countries
- Water
- British Open
- U.S. Open
- PGA

U.S. Open

1. 2018—Shinnecock Hills Golf Club, Shinnecock Hills, New York
2. 2017—Erin Hills, Erin, Wisconsin
3. 2016—Oakmont Country Club, Oakmont, Pennsylvania
4. 2015—Chambers Bay, University Place, Washington
5. 2014—Pinehurst Resort, Course No. 2, Pinehurst, North Carolina
6. 2013—Merion Golf Club, East Course, Ardmore, Pennsylvania

PGA Championship

1. 2018—Bellerive Country Club, St. Louis, Missouri
2. 2017—Quail Hollow Club, Charlotte, North Carolina
3. 2016—Baltusrol Golf Club, Springfield, New Jersey
4. 2015—Whistling Straits, Kohler, Wisconsin
5. 2014—Valhalla Golf Club, Louisville, Kentucky
6. 2013—Oak Hill Country Club, Pittsford, New York

Women in Golf

Although women are not able to play in the Masters Golf Tournament, there are many organizations and tournaments for female golfers. Records show that women have been playing golf since the mid-1500s. In 1867, the first women's golf club, the Ladies' Golf Club, was formed in St Andrews, Scotland. At the time, there were no women playing golf professionally.

In 1893, the Ladies Golf Union of Great Britain decided to have the first British Ladies Golf Championship. Only amateur golfers played in this tournament. Lady Margaret Scott won the first three championships.

By the 1900s, women's golf was becoming quite popular. In the 1920s, women began playing the sport professionally. In 1924, Helen MacDonald signed with Hillerich & Bradsby. She was the first woman to sign a contract with an equipment company.

Ten years later, Helen Hicks was the first woman to promote a manufacturer's products and give golf clinics. She worked with Wilson Sporting Goods.

Helen Hicks started playing professional golf in 1934 and claimed two professional wins. She is one of the original founders of the Ladies Professional Golf Association (LPGA).

In the 1930s, there were only four tournaments open to American women. In 1946, the U.S. Women's Open began. Four years later, the Ladies Professional Golf Association was formed. The LPGA hosted 14 events in its first season. Like the PGA tour for men, the LPGA has a year-round golf tour. By 1952, there were 21 LPGA events. The 2017 LPGA had 34 events, and prizes exceeding $67 million. Important tournaments for women include the LPGA Championship, the U.S. Women's Open, the Women's British Open, and the Kraft Nabisco Championship. The most important golf events for amateur women are the U.S. Women's Amateur and the British Ladies Amateur Championship.

In 1947, Mildred "Babe" Zaharias became the first American woman to win the British Women's Open.

MICHELLE WIE

Michelle Wie was born in Honolulu, Hawai'i, in 1989. At 10 years of age, she became the youngest player ever to qualify for a U.S. Golf Association amateur championship. She won the U.S. Women's Amateur Public Links Championship when she was only 13 years old. This made her the youngest person ever to win an adult USGA championship. Wie turned professional at the age of 15. At 17 years old, Wie earned $20 million in her first year as a professional golfer. She won her first professional tournament in 2009.

Important Moments

There have been more than 75 Masters Golf Tournaments since the first event. Over the years, the tournament has had many historical highlights.

One of the most memorable moments in Masters history was when Jack Nicklaus won his sixth title in 1986. After tournament leader Seve Ballesteros hit the ball into the water on the 15th green, Nicklaus saw his chance to take over the lead. Nicklaus shot the ball over the water, and then sunk the putt for an **eagle**. Nicklaus went on to shoot a **birdie** on both the 16th and 17th holes to beat Tom Kite by one shot.

In 1996, Greg Norman seemed the obvious winner, carrying a six-shot lead into the final round. He needed to shoot a par 72 to win the tournament, but he hit **bogeys** on the 9th through 12th holes. In the end, Norman scored 78, losing to Nick Faldo. Norman is one of the world's best-known golfers, but he has never won a Masters.

Tiger Woods and Chris DiMarco battled for the win in 2005. DiMarco led the tournament at the end of the third round, but Tiger jumped ahead by three strokes in the final nine holes. Tiger had one of the most memorable shots in Masters history on the 16th hole, when he chipped the ball in for a birdie. DiMarco attempted to make a chip on the 18th hole, but he was unsuccessful. In the end, Tiger pulled ahead to win the title. It was his first major win in three years.

Greg Norman came in second in the Masters three times, in 1986, 1987, and 1996. He was inducted into the World Golf Hall of Fame in 2001.

Most tournament-winning scores are under par. In the case of the Masters, this means the golfer takes 288 strokes or fewer during the entire tournament. Over the history of the Masters, only three players have won with a score above par. They were Sam Snead in 1954, Jack Burke Jr. in 1956, and Zach Johnson in 2007. They each took 289 strokes.

The 2018 Masters was the 82nd edition of the tournament. Patrick Reed beat runner-up Rickie Fowler by one stroke, finishing at 15 under par and claiming his first major title.

4
Most Runner-Up Finishes
in the Masters
Ben Hogan, Jack Nicklaus,
Tom Weiskopf

15
Most Top 5 Finishes
Jack Nicklaus

52
years
Most Total
Years Played
Gary Player

21
years old
Youngest Person to
Win a Masters
Tiger Woods

MASTERS
GOLF TOURNAMENT
RECORDS

22
Most Top 10 Finishes
Jack Nicklaus

6
Most wins
Most Wins in the
Masters Tournament
Jack Nicklaus

29
Most Top 25 Finishes
Jack Nicklaus

50
years
Most Consecutive
Years Played
Arnold Palmer

46
years old
Oldest Person to Win
a Masters
Jack Nicklaus

Legends and Current Stars

Arnold Palmer

Arnold Palmer was born in 1929 in Latrobe, Pennsylvania. He is one of the best-known golfers of all time. Palmer began playing golf when he was three years old. He served in the United States Coast Guard from 1950 to 1953. The following year, he won the U.S. Amateur Golf Championship. Palmer decided then to begin his career as a professional golfer. He was the first golfer to win the Masters four times, winning in 1958, 1960, 1962, and 1964. By 1968, Palmer had become the first golfer to earn more than $1 million in tournament prize money. His fans were nicknamed "Arnie's Army." Palmer retired from tournament golf in 2006.

Jack Nicklaus

Jack Nicklaus was born in Columbus, Ohio, in 1940. Some people believe he is the most talented golfer of the 20th century. Nicklaus began golfing at the age of 10. By the time he was 16, Nicklaus had won his first important tournament—the Ohio Open. Between 1959 and 1986, he set a record for the most victories in golf's Grand Slam tournaments, with 18. From 1959 to 1961, Nicklaus won 29 out of 30 of the amateur tournaments he entered. In 1961, Nicklaus became a professional golfer and beat Arnold Palmer that year. This started a rivalry between the two players. Nicklaus won six Masters Golf Tournaments, the most by any player in history. At age 46, he was the oldest winner when he took the title in 1986. He retired from competitive golf in 2005.

Jordan Spieth

Born in 1993 in Dallas, Texas, Jordan Spieth is considered one of the best young golfers currently competing. As a child, Spieth's first love was baseball, but he started focusing on golf at 12 years old and quickly started to gain recognition. He won the U.S. Junior Amateur Championship in 2009 and 2011. Spieth turned professional in 2012 and was named the PGA Rookie of the Year the following year. The young player had a record-breaking year in 2015, which he began by winning the Masters. He shot a 270, tying the 72-hole record of 18 under par. That year, he went on to win the U.S. Open and the Open Championship, and came in second for the PGA Championship. In 2017, he claimed his third major win at the Open Championship. Spieth finished the 2018 Masters two strokes behind winner Patrick Reed, which earned him third place.

Phil Mickelson

Phil Mickelson was born in 1970 in San Diego, California. He began hitting golf balls at 18 months of age. Mickelson golfs left-handed, even though he is right-handed. He learned the game by mirroring the swing of his father, who is a right-handed golfer. Mickelson attended Arizona State University. He won three national college championships. In 1990, he became the first left-handed golfer to win the U.S. Amateur Championship. In the same year, Mickelson won his first professional tournament while still an amateur. He was only the fourth golfer in history to accomplish this feat. Mickelson became a professional golfer in 1992. The following year, he won his first tournament as a pro. Mickelson won his first Masters in 2004. He won the Masters again in 2006 and 2010. Mickelson also won another major tournament, the PGA Championship, in 2005. Mickelson was inducted into the World Golf Hall of Fame in 2012. The following year, he had another major win, when he won the Open Championship.

All-Time Records

253

Justin Thomas finished the 2017 Sony Open with 253 strokes, the lowest number of strokes to complete a 72-hole PGA tournament.

88

Kathy Whitworth claimed the most LPGA Tour wins, with 88 between 1962 and 1985.

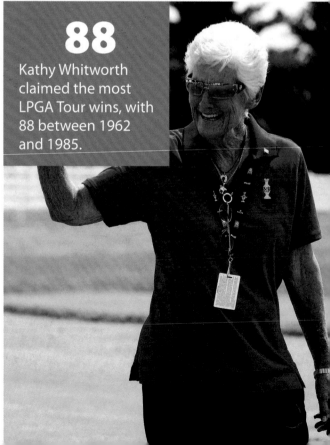

28

Jordan Spieth set the record for most birdies during the Masters in 2015, with 28.

58

Jim Furyk set a PGA Tour record for the lowest score in one round, 58, during the final round of the 2016 Travelers Championship.

82

Between 1936 and 1965, Sam Snead set the record for PGA Tour wins with 82, which includes 3 Masters tournaments.

The Masters Golf Tournament
Timeline

1930

1940

1950

A new season of golf tournaments begins each year with the Masters. The world's best golfers gather to compete for the coveted green jacket, which only one person will earn. The Augusta National Golf Club is continuing its traditions, while also expanding to include a women's championship, in the years to come.

1943 –1945
The tournament ceases play for three years during World War II. The course is used to raise money for the war effort.

1939
The tournament name is officially changed to the Masters Golf Tournament.

1931
Construction begins on the Augusta National Golf Club.

1934
Bobby Jones and Clifford Roberts host the first official tournament at Augusta.

2018
Masters Tournament chairman Fred Ridley announces the creation of the Augusta National Women's Amateur Championship.

2013
Adam Scott wins the Masters on the second hole of sudden death, finishing at 9-under (279). He becomes the first golfer from Australia to win the championship.

TODAY

2010

2000

1990

1980

1997
Tiger Woods becomes the youngest player and first African American to win the Masters.

2002
The National Council of Women's Organizations challenges the no-female members policy of the Augusta National Golf Club.

1980
Seve Ballesteros of Spain wins the Masters to become the first golfer from Europe to win the tournament.

Today
With a long history of excellence, the Masters tournament continues to excite fans with every stroke.

2003
Mike Weir wins the Masters to become the first Canadian to win a major tournament.

1. What year was the first Masters Golf Tournament played?

2. Which player has won the most Masters titles?

3. Who is the youngest person to win the Masters?

4. Where is the Masters played each year?

5. Does the Masters Golf Tournament rotate through different courses each year?

10 QUESTIONS To Test Your Knowledge

6. Besides money, what are the major prizes at this tournament?

7. How many ways can a golfer qualify for the Masters?

8. Are women allowed to play at the Masters?

9. Who is the oldest player to win the title?

10. Name three other major golf tournaments.

ANSWERS

1. 1934
2. Jack Nicklaus
3. Tiger Woods
4. Augusta, Georgia
5. No, it is played every year at the Augusta National Golf Club.
6. The green jacket, the Masters Trophy, and a gold medal
7. 19
8. No, only men
9. Jack Nicklaus, at age 46
10. The U.S. Open, the British Open, and the PGA Championship

Key Words

bent grass: thick grass with shallow roots that is often found in pastures and lawns

Bermuda grass: grass that grows well in poor soil, spreads easily, and recovers well from damage; native to Europe and Africa

birdie: a score of one stroke under par on a hole

blistering: getting small, pus-filled bubbles on the skin that are caused by rubbing

bogeys: scores of one stroke over par on a hole

eagle: a score of two strokes under par on a hole

etiquette: a code of behavior in a particular place

exclusive: only admitting certain people

graphite: a soft black or gray form of carbon

synthetic: human-made

Index

Log on to www.av2books.com

AV² by Weigl brings you media enhanced books that support active learning. Go to www.av2books.com, and enter the special code found on page 2 of this book. You will gain access to enriched and enhanced content that supplements and complements this book. Content includes video, audio, weblinks, quizzes, a slide show, and activities.

AV² Online Navigation

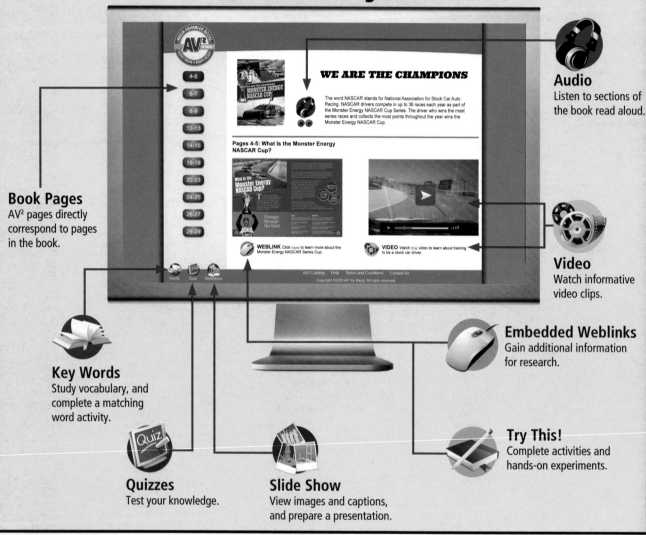

Audio
Listen to sections of the book read aloud.

Book Pages
AV² pages directly correspond to pages in the book.

Video
Watch informative video clips.

Key Words
Study vocabulary, and complete a matching word activity.

Embedded Weblinks
Gain additional information for research.

Try This!
Complete activities and hands-on experiments.

Quizzes
Test your knowledge.

Slide Show
View images and captions, and prepare a presentation.

AV² was built to bridge the gap between print and digital. We encourage you to tell us what you like and what you want to see in the future.

Sign up to be an AV² Ambassador at www.av2books.com/ambassador.

Due to the dynamic nature of the Internet, some of the URLs and activities provided as part of AV² by Weigl may have changed or ceased to exist. AV² by Weigl accepts no responsibility for any such changes. All media enhanced books are regularly monitored to update addresses and sites in a timely manner. Contact AV² by Weigl at 1-866-649-3445 or av2books@weigl.com with any questions, comments, or feedback.